W9-BEL-668

STR
Strickland, Brad.
When Mack came back

DATE DUE 0106134

When Mack Came Back

BRAD STRICKLAND

When Mack Came Back

0106134

Dial Books for Young Readers
New York

Published by Dial Books for Young Readers
A division of Penguin Putnam Inc.
345 Hudson Street
New York, New York 10014

Designed by Nancy R. Leo-Kelly
The text of this book is set in Weiss
Printed in the U.S.A. on acid-free paper
1 3 5 7 9 10 8 6 4 2

Library of Congress Cataloging in Publication Data
Strickland, Brad.
When Mack came back/by Brad Strickland.
p. cm.
Summary: When his older brother Ben leaves the family farm in order
to join the army in 1943, ten-year-old Maury remains behind to
deal with his angry father and to care for Ben's injured puppy.
ISBN 0-8037-2498-5
[1. Dogs—Fiction. 2. Father and sons—Fiction. 3. Farm life—Fiction.
4. United States—History—1933–1945—Fiction.] I. Title.
PZ7.S9166Wh   2000   [Fic]—dc21   99-27772   CIP

For Toby Sherry,
world's finest editor and a great friend

Chapter 1

I heard the ghost in the woods the day before Jimmy Marshall and I played war. My daddy wouldn't let us play war around the house. This was in December of 1943, and he was still mad about my brother Ben's joining the army. Ben was finishing basic training, the last we heard. Afterward he was going to a replacement training camp and then overseas.

That was all I knew. Daddy had stopped getting the newspaper, and he wouldn't even let us listen to the war news on the radio if he was in the room. He sure didn't want me playing war. Once I made him mad by doing something wrong. He'd said, "Maury

Painter, if World War Two goes on another eight years, you'll get to be eighteen and run off just like Ben. That'll prove I got two fools for sons." He just didn't want to hear anything about Ben or about the war.

So I was far out of sight of the house, all the way past the high pasture up on the side of Rocky Hill. The day was gray, with low clouds and the smell of rain in the air. I was figuring how to fight my war with Jimmy. It was my turn to be America and his to be the enemy, and it would be nice to win. I had just found a good spot—a wide crack between two big granite boulders, where it was cool and tight, making me feel as though a giant with hard fingers were holding me. I was squirming out of my hiding place when the ghost began to howl.

Anyway, my first thought was that it was a ghost. The voice was low, kind of hoarse, and awfully mournful. It made the hairs on my arms stand up and my skin crinkle into gooseflesh. *Boo-oo-oo-ooo!*

The sound just froze me. I could no more have run away than I could have flapped my arms and flown over the barn. Then it came again. *Boo-oo-oo-ooo!* The noise wasn't like any animal. And it wasn't Jimmy trying to spook me. Jimmy was such a scaredy-cat that if he tried that, he would've scared his own self.

My heart felt as if it were trying to beat its way right out of my chest.

I stood beside the rocks, listening. The bawling started again. It was coming from up the hill, where tangles of dry, dead blackberry vines coiled under the pines. "Who's there?" I hollered, trying to make my voice big and bold.

For a second nothing happened. Then a dog barked. It was a terrible, rusty-sounding bark, but it was just a bark. And then the dog bellowed again, that mournful, lost-sounding cry.

Feeling less afraid, I started to pick my way up the hill. Halfway to the top a scary thought stopped me. What if it was a mad dog?

This was December, and you didn't often hear about dogs going mad in December. Rabies was a disease that came with the hot summer weather. Still—

The dog bawled from so close that I could see the blackberry vines jerking where it had to be. The sound was so lonesome and sorrowful that it made me forget about mad dogs. I picked up a dead limb and pushed the springy blackberry vines aside. That didn't do me much good. The vines still hooked their thorns into my jeans and into my skin.

The bushes ahead of me shook. I crawled into a

rocky little clearing and hunkered down, sitting on my heels. "Where are you?"

The dog woofed—a sick sound, like a bad cough. I used my limb to push through the blackberry vines, and then saw him, a black pup. He was a mix, but he looked mostly pointer. He was wearing a scratched-up brown collar, and trailing from the collar was a short rope that had tangled around and around the blackberry thorns. It looked like maybe he had crawled in there to sleep and gotten all snarled. He was on his side with the rope wrapped around one front leg. His back was curved, and his hind legs were twisted up under him. Lord knows how long he had been there.

I reached in and felt him. He licked my hand, but his tongue was so dry, it felt like soft sandpaper rasping over my fingers. "It's okay," I said. My brother Ben had owned a dog just like this one. When he had joined the army that past September, he had given it away to a friend who lived on the far side of Guthrie, thirty miles away.

I felt the collar and pulled at the buckle. The dog waited patiently, whimpering and shivering. I tugged and jerked. My thumbnail broke, but at last the collar was loose. "Come on, boy," I said. "Come on out."

The dog wiggled out on his belly. I didn't reckon he had strength to do more than that. My breath caught. He was just skin and bones. His brown eyes were sunk deep into his head, with feverish red eyelids. You could have counted his ribs, easy. He was all black, except for a white blaze on his forehead and down his muzzle. His fur was streaked with mud and briars and snarled with twigs. He breathed hard.

I hunkered there, petting him. He was half grown, maybe six months old. My brother Ben's dog had been three months old when he gave it away. I couldn't hardly see how this could be Ben's dog, but it sure looked like him. Ben had named his dog General MacArthur. That was too much of a mouthful, so we had called him Mack.

"Mack?" I said. "Mack? Is that you?"

The dog's head came up when he heard the name. His tired tail thumped once, twice.

There was something hard in my throat that I couldn't swallow. This was my brother's dog. He had come back home, thirty miles through the woodsy back country of north Georgia. I couldn't guess how he had found the way, or how long he had been on the road.

But from the look of him, he sure wasn't going to

be able to walk to the house. I was going to have to carry him.

At six months, he had a fair size on him, but he was too skinny. I hugged him against my chest with his front paws on my shoulder. The dog licked my left ear with that soft-sandpaper tongue. "We're going home," I said. "Remember me, Mack? I'm Maury. Maury Painter, Ben's brother. I'm taking you home."

Mack sighed, as though he knew he was going to be taken care of now. His breath was sour, but it smelled a little like yeast too, like freshly baked bread. His breathing scared me—a heave and a kind of dry rustle in his chest.

I had to fight my way out of the briars. The hooked spines caught in the dog's coat, and in my clothes, raking bloody lines across my arms. The thin cloth of my shirt ripped more than once. Mama wouldn't like that. She would have to sew up or patch my clothes again.

The hill was steep. I got to the bottom and the barbed-wire fence. There I had to put the dog down. He whined, looking at me with those glassy brown eyes.

"It's all right," I said, and climbed over the fence. Then I coaxed him under the fence and picked him up again. Before long, sweat ran down my face, even though the day was cool. Once a scared rabbit jumped up and went bounding away, white tail high. He leaped through the long grass as though he were on springs. Two of our cows took time out from munching the dry yellow grass to raise their heads and stare at us.

My feet felt as though they weighed ten pounds apiece. By the time I came in sight of the gate and the house, my shoulders were aching and my arms were trembling.

"What you got?" Sissy hollered, running toward me. She was my sister, nearly six years old, and sometimes the most aggravating young'un the Lord ever let live. She was wearing a plaid shirt too big for her and hand-me-down overalls that had been Ben's before they were mine. "What is it? I'm gonna tell on you."

She was always telling on me. Even when I hadn't done hardly anything at all.

"Call Mama," I said, all out of breath.

"I'll get Old Pa."

"Melissa Cecilia Painter! You do as I tell you! Call Mama!" I hollered after her as she ran toward the house. Mama would be better with a sick dog than Daddy or Old Pa would. Mama had a tender heart about animals. Daddy would probably say the dog was too far gone and might even shoot him. Old Pa would go on about how we couldn't afford to feed any dog.

But with Mama it might be different. She used to teach school before she married Daddy, and she hated to see suffering. The door slammed behind Sissy, and I got through the gate, hoping that when the door opened again, it wouldn't be Old Pa or Daddy.

It did open when I was halfway across the yard, dodging the white chickens and staggering with the weight of that dog.

I breathed easier.

Mama stood in the doorway, her hand covering her mouth. Her blue eyes were wide and shocked.

Maybe the dog had a chance.

Chapter 2

Daddy said, "I don't think that's Ben's dog."

Mack thumped his tail once. He was lying on an old rag rug in the corner of the kitchen. He had been there nearly a week, ever since the day I'd found him on Rocky Hill. The dog wasn't getting any better. "It's Mack," I said.

"Then he don't belong here anymore," Daddy said. He turned away. His shadow fell across Mack and me. Daddy was a tall, skinny man, and he had the same big nose that Ben had. Daddy wasn't even forty-five then, but his hair was already gray. He generally wore a hat all year around, but Mama had finally broken him of wearing it indoors.

Daddy walked over to the fireplace and stood leaning on the mantel. Six hickory logs snapped and crackled in the fire and filled the kitchen with their scent. It always made me think of summer barbecues, even in the dead of winter. "You cut some wood for your mama?" Daddy asked me as he put another log on the fire.

"Yes, sir," I said, watching the red sparks fly up the chimney like angels in a hurry to get to heaven. It was Christmas Eve. Around Christmastime is when you're good anyway, but I was being extra good. Splitting big piles of firewood and stove wood had left both my hands blistered. We had a large stack of it now, enough to last us clear into the new year.

School was out, but every morning I got up early and milked our cows and fed the chickens and collected the eggs. I'd even churned butter, and that's about the most boring job there is. Mama had said, "You must want something special for Christmas to be this good."

My answer was that all I wanted for Christmas was for Mack to stay and get well.

"Don't you still want that bicycle?" Mama had asked.

"No'm," I had said. "I just want Mack to be my dog."

Now he lay on his side, still breathing hard. Every once in a while he would gasp and gulp, as if he were hurting inside. And though he drank a lot of water, he hardly ate anything. His eyes were still sunken, and his ribs still stuck out. I petted him and told him he would be all right.

Old Pa came in. He had been feeding the hogs. As he stood at the sink washing his hands with the gritty Lava soap, he asked, "That dog still alive?"

"Yes, sir," I said. "He's getting better."

Old Pa came over and hooked his thumbs in his overall galluses. "No he ain't," he declared, looking down. He turned to Daddy and said, "John, this dog needs some doctoring."

Daddy shook his head. "Don't have the money for Doc Varney," he said. "Ain't going to owe him."

That was how Daddy lived. Make your own way in life. Don't owe anybody anything. Old Pa couldn't complain about that. He was my daddy's daddy, and he had raised him that way. "All right, John, but that dog's pretty sick," he tried again. For a few seconds they stood looking at each other. Old Pa looked just like Daddy, except his hair was white. Same big Painter nose. Same stubborn mouth and blue eyes. Ben had them too.

"I wasn't the one brought the dog in," Daddy said

at last. "You know how tight things are right now. There just ain't any money for doctoring up a dog, and that's all there is to it."

"John, all I said was the dog is sick," Old Pa told him from the doorway. He went on out.

"He'll have to get better by himself," Daddy said in his short way. "Or if he don't, I can take my shotgun and put him out of his misery."

That kind of talk made me feel sick. Daddy had shot a mule of ours once, back when I was littler than Sissy. The mule had broken its leg, and Daddy took his rifle out to the barn and killed it. Then he hooked the tractor to the mule's body and hauled it off for burial. So I knew he wasn't joking. If he thought Mack was getting worse, he just might put him out of his misery.

"Daddy," I asked, "how much would it cost for Doc Varney to look at Mack?"

"More than you've got," he said.

He was probably right. Upstairs in my bedroom I had a pint Ball fruit jar with some pennies, nickels, and dimes in it. The last time I had counted, two dollars and sixteen cents were in that jar. I didn't know how much a vet charged to look at a sick dog, but once Doc Varney had come out when a calf was sick. That had cost Daddy ten dollars.

When Daddy left the kitchen, I went to the ice-box. Behind the milk jug I had hidden a piece of ham, saving it for Mack. I brought it over to him and started to pinch off little bites. "Here," I said. "It's good."

Mack's tail thumped. He sniffed the ham. He ate three tiny pieces, but then he wouldn't eat the fourth.

"You have to eat, boy," I told him softly.

Mama had doctored us both the day Mack came home. The pads of Mack's feet had been all ragged and bloody, as if he'd walked for miles over sharp rocks. They had left rusty streaks on the shoulders of my shirt. Mama washed Mack's paws and dabbed iodine on them, and although Mack shivered, he didn't cry. "Oh, my land," she had said when she had me strip off my shirt and saw where the thorns had hooked me. I had long bloody stripes across both arms and over my chest.

She had painted them brownish-red with iodine too, and it made me yelp once or twice, it stung so. Then she had fixed up the rug in the corner for Mack, and he'd been there beside the wood box ever since.

Sissy came in. "Santy Claus comes tonight," she told me.

"I know it," I said to her.

13

"I'm going to get a dolly," she said.

"I hope you do."

"Is your dog better?" she asked.

I shrugged. "I think he is," I answered, but really, Mack seemed worse, if anything.

That evening after supper, I helped Mama wash the dishes. "How much would it take to call the doctor for Mack?" I asked as I dried a glass.

She shook her head. "I don't know, Maury. Maybe if he's not better in a few days, I'll ask your father about it."

That evening we sang some Christmas carols around the fireplace—"Silent Night" and "The First Noel" and "Joy to the World." Then Old Pa said a Christmas prayer, and, one by one, we all chimed in. Daddy said, "Lord, look after our Ben when he goes to foreign lands."

Mama prayed that the new year would be a good one and that it would bring peace.

Sissy prayed that she would get her doll.

When it was my turn, I said, "Lord, if it's all right with you, please help Mack get better."

When I opened my eyes, Daddy was staring at me, his eyes hard. "Maury, don't you mock the Lord," he said to me. "It's not His business to worry over a dog. Not when the whole world is at war."

We all went to bed. My bedroom was upstairs. Until Ben left, we shared it. Now Ben's bed was where I threw my schoolbooks, baseball bat, and other things. The weather had turned cold. I got undressed in a hurry, tossing my clothes on top of the mess on Ben's bed, and scooted under the sheets and quilts. My room was always chilly in cold weather, and when it got way below freezing, Mama made a pallet on the kitchen floor so I could sleep in front of the fire.

But this wasn't five-degrees-below-zero cold, it was just Christmas cold. Before long, the bed warmed up some. I lay on my side, covered except for my face. The night sky outside the window was a kind of blue-black. The stars gleamed like the white sparks that flew when the blacksmith was making a shoe for one of our mules. I said my prayer again and again, just in case God had been too busy to hear it the first time. Finally sleep came.

Chapter 3

Jimmy Marshall's house had a parlor, but our house had just a front room. That was where we put up our Christmas tree. Three days before Christmas, Daddy had gone into the woods and found the tree, a straight, full pine about as tall as I was. He had nailed two crosspieces of wood to the bottom of the sawed-off trunk and stood the tree up in front of the window, and his part was finished.

Mama and Sissy and I did all the rest. First we strung twisted strands of red and white crepe paper on the mantel.

Mama had made a tree skirt out of quilted red and green cloth, and she had embroidered the words *Merry Christmas* on it. While Sissy and I hung our stockings on the mantel, she put the skirt around the bottom of the tree. We had just one string of lights—red, yellow, white, blue, and green. That went on the tree. Then we had popped popcorn and strung it. Sissy had stuck me twice with her needle, making out like it was an accident. I didn't even yell at her, because I was being good.

We had hung the popcorn strings and the silver and gold balls that Mama kept all year in the top of her closet. Finally Mama had put the angel on the top. The angel wore a silver dress, and she had her hands clasped in front of her.

"When Ben was about Sissy's age, he said that was the prettiest woman in the world," Mama had told us. "He said he was going to find a woman like that when he grew up and marry her."

"Maybe he'll marry a foreign lady," Sissy had said.

Mama had started to cry.

Now it was Christmas morning. Sissy woke me up scratching on my door. "Get up," she whispered. "Get *up*."

I opened my eyes. The window was just barely

gray. "It's not even daylight," I told her.

"Get up," Sissy said again. "I want to see if Santy Claus came."

It wasn't any use telling her to let me alone. She would keep on until she woke up Mama and Daddy and made Daddy mad. So I got up and got my clothes off Ben's bed. They were stiff with cold. I got my socks and shoes on and opened the door. Sissy was still in her nightgown, shivering and barefoot. "You go get your clothes on," I told her. "And put something on your feet. You're going to get pneumonia."

"I want to see if Santy Claus came first," she said.

"I won't build a fire until you start to get dressed," I warned her.

"You're mean," she whined.

"Melissa Cecilia Painter, you go get some clothes on."

Finally she went back into her room, across the landing from Ben's and mine. I went downstairs, taking it easy on the squeaky step. Mama and Daddy slept in one of the two downstairs bedrooms, and Old Pa slept in the other one. In the kitchen, Mack lay so still that my heart stopped for a second. He looked dead.

Then he raised his head and blinked at me. His tail wagged once.

"Poor old boy," I said. "Cold in here. A fire will warm you."

A little hatchet was in the wood box. There was some fat wood, sticks of pine that burned easily. I split them into small strips of kindling that smelled sharp and clean, like turpentine. The kindling caught with the first match, and then some heavier sticks of pine went over them. When that caught with a sizzle and a hiss of pine rosin, I stacked some small pieces of hickory on top. Then the front-room fire had to be started the same way. The wood snapped and popped as it caught fire. The big clock above the mantel ticked. Six minutes past six o'clock. I kept myself from looking at the tree. Sissy would never forgive me if she didn't get to see the presents first.

When the front-room fire was burning, I went back to the kitchen and poured a little bowl of milk for Mack. He took a couple of laps at it, then groaned.

My chest felt tight. I couldn't fool myself. Mack wasn't getting any better. He was getting worse.

Sissy came downstairs in the most ungodly get-up

I had ever seen. She had put on an old pink dress that was too little for her, and then she had pulled on some overalls. She was wearing one black shiny shoe that she wore to church, and one black P. F. Flyers tennis shoe. The end of the sneaker had a big hole in it, and her toes poked through. "You look like a clown," I told her.

She stuck out her tongue at me. I followed her into the front room. "Oh, Maury," she said. She reached for my hand and squeezed it.

Our Christmas stockings were bulging with oranges, apples, pecans, and Brazil nuts. But that wasn't what she was looking at. Under the tree was a wooden cradle. In the cradle was a baby doll with golden hair, wrapped up in a pink blanket.

And beside the cradle was a boy's bicycle. It wasn't new. The handlebars had little spots of rust on the underside. Both the tires looked slick. But somebody had painted the bike with shiny blue paint. Somebody else had made a quilted blue cloth cover for the old seat. "I got my bike," I said.

"And I got a dolly and a cradle too," Sissy told me. She ran over to the tree, knelt down, and rocked the cradle.

I had to smile at her. "Those elves at the North Pole do a good job."

Sissy tucked the blanket around her doll. "They can carve too. My cradle is just as good as anything Old Pa could make."

Mama came in, wearing her pink chenille housedress. "Is that what you wanted?" she asked us.

"I have a baby," Sissy said.

"Yes'm," I said, lying.

That year Christmas came on Saturday. After breakfast, Mama bundled us up and we rode in the wagon to Hopewell Methodist Church. Not many people were there for the special service, and it was an extra-short sermon. We were back home before noon.

After lunch, I asked to go out and ride my bike some. Daddy said to go, but to be careful. Mama added that if I wanted to go with everybody over to Woodbine to see Aunt Mary, to come back in an hour. I knew they would hitch up the mules again and ride in the wagon. Daddy didn't drive the truck when he could help it because he had only an A ration sticker. That meant he couldn't buy very much gas. I really wouldn't mind missing the trip. It took us a long time to get to Aunt Mary's when we went in the wagon. And at her house, there was nothing to do. Aunt Mary made me sit still and be quiet.

I rolled my bike out onto the front porch and bounced it down the steps. I knew how to ride a bike. My friends had let me learn on theirs. All morning I had been thinking about my destination.

Frankie Carter lived about six miles from us, toward Guthrie, the town where Daddy sold his produce. Frankie never got any toys for Christmas. He got money instead. His daddy and mama wanted him to go to college to be a doctor, and they made him save his money. I thought somebody would have to be pretty sick to want to be doctored by Frankie Carter. He was a big, heavy, goofy-looking kid. Every time you saw him, he had his finger up his nose, picking away. And he was always borrowing stuff from other people in school and never giving it back.

I rode along the dirt road, going at a pretty good clip. The bike was a little old, but it worked well. The chain was freshly oiled, and the coaster brake felt nice and tight. I whizzed along under a bright blue sky with the Christmas sun in my face. Sometimes in the hollows the wheels crunched over hoarfrost that stuck up out of the red earth. Before long I was pretending to be an American pilot, flying my P-40 fighter plane out on patrol. My nose started to tingle with the chilly wind.

Frankie's house looked nicer than ours. Ours was bare, weathered wood, but Frankie's was painted white, and the windows had dark green trim. I pulled up in his yard, breathing hard. He answered the door himself. "Merry Christmas," I told him.

"Merry Christmas yourself," Frankie echoed in his squeaky voice. "What did you get?"

"Some clothes and stuff," I said. "How about you?"

"I got a Barlow knife," he answered. "And a pocket watch. And twenty-five dollars."

"I got a bike," I said. "You want to ride it?"

Frankie's eyes lit up. He didn't have a two-wheeler. That was because his mama worried that Frankie would get killed on a bike. Mrs. Carter was kind of scared about things.

A long time back, Frankie's older brother had died when he was five or six years old. It was some kind of accident. I never did know just what had happened. Frankie told different stories. Sometimes his brother had been hit by a truck, and sometimes an airplane had crashed on top of him. It had happened a long time before Frankie was even born, so maybe he didn't know.

Anyway, I had watched my daddy trade cars two or three times. It was clear that Frankie loved the bike. You could see from the way he swooped it down the hill in front of his house that he was doing the same thing I had done, pretending to be a pilot in the Army Air Corps. Pretty soon we got to talking. At first he said he couldn't offer more than five, but he came up to six, then to seven. After about ten minutes, we shook hands on the deal. Then I began the long walk to Guthrie.

Five miles isn't much in a car, or even when you're on a bike. But it's a weary way when you're on foot. The walk takes a lot longer than an hour. I plodded along a dirt road with high red banks. My feet were cold and my nose felt frozen. Nobody passed me. Crows screamed from the pine trees. Once in a while a rabbit would take off through the underbrush beside the road. I crossed the old wooden bridge over Five Mile Creek and saw that the rocks in the creek bed were all glazed with ice. My knees began to ache, the way they do after a bad fall. My nose was running, and my breath drifted away in a white cloud.

It was hard not to think about what Daddy was going to say. He loved us all, but that meant he was awfully strict sometimes. Once, a year or two before, he had found me sitting in one of the apple trees behind the house, reading a book. "There's work to be done," he had told me. "You need to be less like your mama and more like your brother if you want to be a farmer."

Well, there it was. I didn't want to be a farmer, not really. Ben was good at the same things Daddy liked: plowing, planting, hoeing, harvesting. It didn't upset Ben to butcher a hog or to wring a chicken's neck. Both those things bothered me. I could help out after the hog was killed, or even pluck the feathers off a chicken. But killing them made me feel bad, as if my insides were scrunched up.

Reading was what I liked, but Daddy didn't see much sense in it. To him, his older son was the one who knew how to be a farmer. His younger one— me—disappointed him a little. And here I was, about to disappoint him again. Still, Mack deserved a chance. Maybe there would be some way to make it all up to Daddy later.

After walking a long time, I began to pass houses, and then the houses were closer and closer together, and the road became a paved street.

Finally, when it was almost three in the afternoon, I got to town. Guthrie has about a dozen stores, a couple of gas stations, and the brick school where the town kids go. Doc Varney lived in town, in the same house where he had his veterinary clinic.

A woman answered my knock on the door. It must

have been Mrs. Varney, though I hadn't ever seen her. She was a pretty lady with neat brown hair. She was wearing a navy blue dress and white beads, as if she had just come back from church. "Yes?" she asked, smiling at me and kind of tilting her head.

"Is Doctor Varney at home?" I asked her.

She had me come into the parlor. I didn't know there were any such rooms in the world, outside of the picture show. A glass chandelier glimmered in the center of the room. It seemed to have a dozen bulbs. Back home, our electric lights hung down on cords from the ceiling, and you turned them on by pulling a chain. These had buttons in the walls. And a Christmas tree in the corner went all the way up to the ceiling. It had hundreds of lights, their glow reflected by bunches of silver icicles. Red candles were positioned on the mantel, with boughs of holly between them. I stood there blinking, the scent of cedar and holly in my nearly frozen nose.

Doc Varney walked in, wearing a black vest and britches and a polka-dotted blue bow tie. He was a short, bald-headed man, his eyes big behind thick round spectacles. "Yes?" he asked me.

I cleared my throat. "Sir, I'm Maury Painter. John Painter's boy, from out on Fox Road. It's Christmas, and I hate to bother you, but I have a sick dog."

"A sick dog?" he said after me.

"Yes, sir." I felt in my pockets. "I've got twelve dollars and a little more to pay you with. About a dollar and a half is in pennies, though." And ten dollars was in a crisp new ten-dollar bill. It's what Frankie had paid me for the bike.

"Come on," Doc Varney said. "We'll take my car."

Chapter 4

When we got to the farm, everyone was gone. Mama had left a note stuck on the back door: "We are going to see Aunt Mary for Christmas. You will find some chicken in the icebox."

We went in the house, and while I poked up the fire and put on some fresh logs, Doc Varney bent over Mack. The dog groaned softly. Finishing with the fire, I stood behind the vet. "He hasn't been eating much," I said.

"No wonder," Doc Varney told me. "This dog has a twist in his gut. You say you found him tangled up in some bushes?"

"Yes, sir."

"He probably hurt himself trying to break free." I swallowed hard. "Is he going to die?"

"Maybe not." The doctor started to roll Mack gently over. He put one hand on the dog's stomach and felt it. "I could operate, but he's pretty weak. It would be better if I could just untwist it."

For ten or fifteen minutes he worked on Mack, rolling him around and kneading his belly. Then Mack whimpered. He turned over, got to his feet, and staggered to the kitchen door. Our back porch was low, but Mack had some trouble getting down the two steps. The hens in the yard clucked in worried voices when they saw him. One, a black speckled hen that Sissy called Miss Priss, gabbled so fast it sounded like she was saying, "What-what-what— WHAT?" The chickens didn't need to fret. Mack just ignored them.

Walking with shaky steps, he went over to the fence and did his business. Doc Varney put his hand on my shoulder. "He just might be all right now."

When Mack had finished, Doc Varney went over and looked at what Mack had left on the grass. The vet used a magnifying glass. Then he stood up and came back to where Mack and I stood. "Is he going to get well?" I asked.

"We'll see. He doesn't have worms, anyway. Does your mama have any rice?"

"Yes, sir."

We got a fire going in the black iron cookstove, and Doc Varney rolled up his sleeves. He boiled some rice, and he boiled two eggs. He had me strip some meat off the cold chicken in the icebox and chop it up fine. It was strange to see a man at the stove. Mama always did the cooking. I couldn't even imagine my daddy or Old Pa cooking anything, but the doctor acted as though he were right at home there.

When the rice and the eggs were done, Doc Varney chopped up the eggs and stirred them and the chicken into the rice. "Let's let that cool," he said, taking the pot outside and setting it down on the back porch. Then the doctor came back. "Hold him," he said. "Might as well give him his shots."

Mack was the best dog you ever saw. He didn't cry or even whine when the doctor stuck him. After a while, Doc Varney sent me outside to get the rice and chicken. It was cool enough, so he spooned about a cupful into Mack's bowl. Mack sniffed it, then licked it. Finally Mack gobbled it down, his black tail wagging. "He's eating," I said.

"Eating better?" the vet asked.

"Yes, sir," I said. "A whole lot better." Mack finished off every speck of the food, then licked the plate and looked up.

"Begging for more," the doctor said with a little laugh. "Mack's going to be fine now. Poor pup, he was hurting there for a while. But now he'll be all right."

The doctor gave Mack a little more of the rice and chicken mix and told me to feed Mack again at night. He also gave me a list of things that Mack could eat and some pills he had to take. Doc Varney said he would like to see Mack again in two weeks.

"How much do I owe you?" I asked the vet, the same way my daddy asked the clerk when we bought things at the store.

Doc Varney pulled at his nose. He looked at Mack then at me. "Well, it's Christmas Day," he said. "Why don't we call this a Christmas gift?"

I looked down. "No, sir," I said.

"It's my gift to you," the doctor said.

"No, sir. That wouldn't be right."

The doctor shook his head. "You're John Painter's son, all right. You've got the Painter stubborn streak. Why is it so important to you to pay me?"

"Because it's my dog, and I was the one who came to get you. And because it's my money too." I told him about selling my bike to pay him.

The doctor thought all that over. He nodded. "Well, that changes things then," he said in his serious voice. "Let me see. How much did you say you had in change?"

I didn't rightly remember. We sat down and I dumped the change from my pocket onto the kitchen table. The tablecloth was red-and-white checked. We stacked the pennies in groups of ten, as if they were checkers on a board. The change made sixteen columns, with one penny left over. "There's a dollar and sixty-one cents in pennies," I said. Eight of the pennies were the new kind, the ones made of steel coated with silvery zinc. One of them was an old Indian-head.

I counted the dimes and the nickels. There were three dimes and five nickels. That was fifty-five cents. Fifty-five cents plus a dollar and sixty-one cents made two dollars and sixteen cents exactly.

"You added that up in your head," Doc Varney told me.

"Yes, sir. It's not hard."

"How are you at reading?" he asked.

I thought about it. "I like to read," I answered. "But not schoolbooks so much. Not as much as other books."

"What other books?"

Why did Doc Varney want to know? My teacher, Miss Wilson, was always on me about that. She thought I should read my schoolbooks more and not read the others so much. "Well," I said, "there's *Ivanhoe*, by Sir Walter Scott, and *King Solomon's Mines*, by H. Rider Haggard. I get them from the school library. Mrs. Gould—she's the librarian—won't let you bring them home, but you can keep them in your desk. I was reading *The White Company* by Sir Arthur Conan Doyle when school let out for Christmas. I mean to finish it when we start again."

"What grade are you in, son?" Doc Varney asked me.

"Fourth grade, sir." Most ten-year-olds were in fifth grade, but my birthday was in October. I was nearly seven when I started first grade, and about the tallest one in my room.

"You keep up your reading and your 'rithmetic," the doctor said. "Some day you will be glad you did."

"Yes, sir," I said. I didn't know what he meant. I was glad to read already.

I looked down at the stacks of change. "Sir," I said, "how much do I owe you?"

"Well, I always need pennies and small change in my business," Doc Varney told me. "I'll settle for two dollars and fifteen cents, if you let me have a lot of pennies."

"Yes, sir!" Shoot, the doctor needed pennies and nickels and dimes. I could have kept my bike.

The doctor picked up the piles of pennies, then the nickels and dimes. I kept the one odd penny, the old Indian-head. Ben had given it to me. He said it was a lucky piece. Maybe it had brought me some good luck, because now it looked like Mack was going to get well.

I walked Doc Varney out to his car. He shook my hand and told me to take good care of Mack. "He's a fine dog," he told me. "You be a good master to him."

"I'll try, sir," I said.

Doc Varney got into his car, a 1937 Ford, painted black but dull with the dust of dirt roads. The vet waved and backed the car out. Then he drove away. Red dust hung in the air behind him.

I went back inside and sat down at the table. Mack got up from the corner. He walked over to me and put his chin on my knee. Mack looked up at me, brown eyes clear and shining. I patted his head. "Good boy," I told him. "You're going to be all right. Good boy."

Mack sighed. He looked right happy, as if he

knew at last that he was home. Then the dog belched.

I got up to fill his bowl with water. Mack walked right behind me and took four or five laps. I sat down on the hearth with the fire hot on my back. Mack came over and lay down next to me, his head in my lap again.

Times like this, the house could get lonesome. I could hear the hickory wood burning behind me. In the front room the big Regulator clock was ticking loudly. I wondered what Daddy would say when he found out that I had sold my bike. He wouldn't be happy.

But I could worry about all that after Daddy and the others got back from Aunt Mary's. Until then I could just sit warm by the fire and pet my dog.

Chapter 5

Mama, Old Pa, Daddy, and Sissy got back about dark. Mama came in first. She took off her coat and started to say something. She looked at Mack, and then back at me. "He's better," she said. She hung her coat on one of the pegs beside the kitchen door.

"Yes'm," I told her.

Mama came over to where Mack and I sat in front of the kitchen fire. She knelt down and petted him. He wagged his tail and tried to wash her face with his tongue. She laughed and held him off. "He's going to get well," she said, sounding almost as if she were about to cry.

Daddy, Old Pa, and Sissy came in from putting the mules in the barn. Daddy and Old Pa hung their coats up beside Mama's. "Look, John," Mama said. "Look at the dog."

Daddy pushed his hat back on his head. "What's the matter with him?"

Mama laughed. "Nothing. He looks as good as new."

Mack got up from where he sat and walked over to Daddy. He stood at Daddy's feet, wagging his tail and gazing up into Daddy's face. Daddy stared at Mack. "That might be Ben's dog," he said. "It might be the same dog at that."

Old Pa slowly leaned over to pet Mack. " 'Course he is," he said. "You can tell." Mack licked Old Pa's wrinkly hand.

Daddy turned away and took off his hat. "Then Maury will have to take him back to his owner," he stated. He hung his hat on a peg.

"John," Mama said.

"Ben gave that dog away," Daddy said. "If it's really the same dog, he don't belong to us."

"John, the dog came back home," Mama said patiently.

"This ain't his home," Daddy said. His tone of voice said the subject was closed.

"What is this?" Old Pa asked. He had picked up the vet's little medicine bottle from the table.

"Doc Varney left that," I said.

Daddy looked at me long and hard. He fixed his face in a frown. "Doc Varney?"

"Yes, sir," I whispered. My heart was beating as fast as it did when I'd been running for a long time. I took a big swallow. "I asked him to come. Mack was real sick. Doc said he could have died. But he fixed Mack up and gave him his shots too."

"I can't pay a vet bill for a stray dog," Daddy told me.

The way his blue eyes glared at me made me feel small. But I looked right back and said, "No, sir. You won't have to pay a vet bill. Doc Varney's been paid."

"Who paid him?" Daddy asked. He wouldn't stop staring at me. His eyes were angry.

Mama and Old Pa stood behind Daddy. They glanced at each other. Mama seemed sad. I lowered my head. "I paid him."

Daddy wouldn't let go. "Where did you get the money?" he asked. "It takes money to pay a vet bill. Where did you get it?"

"I sold my bike," I mumbled.

Daddy took a step forward. He was so close to me

that I could smell the mothball scent of his Sunday suit. Daddy put his hand on my head and tilted it back so I was looking up at him. "What did you say? Speak up like a man so I can hear you."

I took a big breath. "I sold my bike, sir," I told him. Daddy's face turned pale. He pressed his lips together. I thought he was going to yell at me.

"John," Old Pa said softly, "the bike was his'n."

"Pa, I'm talking to my son," Daddy said.

"And *I'm* talking to *my* son," Pa told him. "I remember the time you sold your pony. You weren't much older than Maury. I didn't whip you, did I?"

Daddy didn't answer Old Pa. "I thought you wanted a bicycle," he said to me.

"Yes, sir, I did," I answered.

"Well," he said, "bicycles aren't easy to get. There's a war on. You said you wanted your own bicycle, and Santa brought you one."

"I did want a bike, sir," I said. "But I wanted my dog to live more."

"John, it was his bicycle," Old Pa said again.

Daddy turned away from me. "I know the bicycle was his'n," he said. His voice was still rough. "If the boy wants to be a fool, then he's going to be a fool. But I am not going to buy his bicycle back. He's going to have to do without."

"That's all right," I told him.

"Who did Ben give the dog to?" Daddy asked Mama. "What was his name?"

"Junior Cowart," Mama said. "John, the dog came here because this is home. We ought to let him stay."

"I won't keep another man's dog," Daddy told her. "Tomorrow we're taking that dog to the Cowart place. He's their dog, and they can have him back."

"He'll just come home again," I told Daddy.

"Then they'll have to keep him chained," Daddy said.

I started to say something else, but Old Pa caught my eye and shook his head. So I went upstairs to my room instead. Mack followed me. He was still shaky on the stairs, but he stayed right behind me. He lay down beside my bed and wagged his tail.

That evening when Mama called me to supper, I told her I wasn't hungry. I heard Daddy say, "Let him sulk, see what good it does him."

I wasn't sulking, just lying there thinking about Mack. One thing Daddy never did was to chain a dog. Old Pa didn't either. We didn't have any dogs on the place now, except Mack. Just Pumpkin and Squirrel, our two cats. I remembered when Daddy had two hunting dogs, though. He never chained them up. Old Pa had once told me you could always tell a mean man. He was the man who would keep a hunting dog on a chain.

I didn't want anybody to do that to Mack. It hurt to imagine him tied to a post or a tree. "I won't let them do it," I whispered. Mack wagged his tail.

I still had the ten dollars left. I would go with Daddy to the Cowart farm. Maybe Junior Cowart would take ten dollars for Mack. If he wouldn't, maybe I could work to make more money. But whatever happened, I would ask Junior Cowart not to put Mack on a chain.

Someone knocked at my door. I knew it was Mama. Daddy never knocked. "Come in," I said.

Mama opened the door. She had a plate of food. "Here's the last of the chicken," she said. "I brought some creamed sweet corn and green beans. And a glass of milk."

"I ain't hungry," I muttered.

"Maury," she said.

I sat up on my bed. "I'm sorry," I told her. "I mean, I'm not hungry, thank you."

Mama sat on the foot of my bed. She gave me the glass and I took a sip of the milk. It was good.

"I didn't mean your grammar," Mama said. "Maury, your father isn't angry at you."

"He sure acts like it," I said. The chicken leg was a little cold, but it was good too. I took a bite of the corn and some of the beans.

Mama smoothed my hair back. "I know your father seems angry. But he isn't mad at you, Maury. When Ben ran off and joined the army, it just about broke his heart."

"Yes'm," I said, eating as though I were starved. I couldn't help it. Mama was a great cook. "I was sad when Ben left too. And you and Sissy and Old Pa were. But you all don't act hateful, the way Daddy does."

"It might have hurt him more than it did us," Mama said. "Your father and Ben are a lot alike. They've got the big Painter nose and the big Painter stubbornness. Ben knew he would soon be drafted into the army. But your father hoped he wouldn't enlist, that he would wait until the army called him. Maybe the war would end. Maybe the army would decide it didn't need Ben. But Ben couldn't wait. What your father can't forgive is that Ben just left before daylight one morning without saying good-bye. We didn't hear from him for a week."

"Mama," I said, "can you ask Daddy to let Mack stay here?"

"Yes," she said. She smiled. "I'm not a Painter,

though. I just married one. The same kind of stubbornness isn't in me."

"Mack could be a hunting dog," I said. "He could help Daddy hunt rabbits or squirrels, and earn his keep."

She took the empty plate from me. "I'll try," she promised.

"Mama . . .," I began.

She stood in the doorway. "Yes, Maury?"

"Mack could be here when Ben gets back," I whispered. "That would make Ben feel at home. He wouldn't ever leave again."

Mama turned her face away. I knew she was crying.

"Mama?" I said.

"It isn't you," Mama told me. She closed the door.

I lay back on the bed, wanting to cry myself. Mack put his front paws on the bed and looked into my face.

"It's all right, boy," I said. But I didn't really think it was.

Chapter 6

The next morning was cold and dark. The sky was full of low, streaky clouds that looked as if they had been painted with a brush. I hoped that Daddy wouldn't remember about Mack, but he did.

After church Daddy said, "Maury, go get old Belle's collar. It's hanging on the wall in the little room."

Mama gave me a sad look and shook her head. I knew it wouldn't do any good to argue. "Yes, sir," I said.

Old Pa once told me the little room used to be a porch. Now it was where Mama kept her round washing machine when she wasn't using it. That took up most of the space. Years ago, Old Pa had papered the walls with newspapers. Sometimes when it was warm I liked to go into the little room and read the old newspapers on the walls. They told of things that had happened in 1919. The whole room was like a history book.

But Daddy had sent me to get a collar that used to belong to Belle, a hunting dog that I could barely remember. She had died when I was younger than Sissy. Her collar was still there, hanging on a nail. I took it down. The leather felt cold and stiff.

I went back inside and handed the collar to Daddy. "Go get the dog," he said.

Mack was in the yard. Pumpkin, the big lazy orange cat, was up on a fence post frowning at him. Mack had his head tilted sideways. I think he wanted to play. "Come here, boy," I said. My throat was hurting. Mack walked over to me. I hugged him, and he followed me up onto the porch.

Daddy came out, wearing his coat. He said, "Put the collar on him. You can come with me if you want."

I knew Mama must have said something to him. I went inside to get my coat. Mama said, "Maury, if that's not Ben's dog, your father says you can keep him."

"Yes'm," I said. I knew that Mack had to be Ben's dog. No other dog would have tried so hard to get home. My heart felt heavy in my chest.

Daddy was cranking up the old truck. It took four or five tries, because he didn't drive it much. He had tied a piece of rope to the dog's collar, and Mack sat on the front seat next to the window. I sat between the dog and Daddy.

We didn't talk much. It took a long time to drive to the Cowart place. We had to go all the way to Guthrie, then along a narrow dirt road that wound through several little towns: Willow Branch, Post Corners, Tynerville. Finally we came to a silver mailbox with the name COWART painted in red letters.

The farmhouse was small. Wood smoke poured out of the chimney. Daddy stopped the truck, and we got out. The ten-dollar bill was in my pocket. I was afraid that Daddy would be mad when I asked Junior Cowart to sell Mack to me.

Daddy knocked on the door. After a while, a woman opened it. She wasn't old, but she wasn't young. Her face looked tired, with washed-out brown eyes and dull brown hair. She wore a faded blue housedress and slippers. "Yes?" she asked, standing in the doorway.

Daddy took off his hat. "I'm John Painter, from yonder side of Guthrie," he said. "Is Junior Cowart here?"

"No, he ain't," the woman said. "Junior's been drafted. He's away off in Kentucky, being trained. I'm Sally, his wife."

Daddy didn't say anything for a second. Then he motioned to me to come up beside him. "Is this here Junior's dog?" he asked her.

The woman frowned at Mack. "He looks like the one somebody gave Junior," she said. "But, Lord, that dog run off in November, one week after Junior reported to the army. I had him tied in the yard, and he chewed through the rope."

"Well," Daddy said, "my boy Ben gave the dog to Junior, and he came back to us. So we're returning him to you."

Sally Cowart shook her head. "Mr. Painter, I'll tell you the truth. I never did want no dog. I can't take care of myself and my baby, hardly, let alone no dog."

"You don't want him?" Daddy asked, surprised.

Mrs. Cowart shook her head again. "I'd have to give him away. If it's the same to you, just keep the dog. He traveled all the way back to your place, so he must like it there."

The hardest thing I have ever done was not to grin all over my face. I just stood there, holding that rope, trying to look solemn and serious. Mack stood next to me, leaning on my leg.

Daddy's face was a sight. I could tell that he had never expected this. He might have thought that Mack wasn't Junior Cowart's dog. He even told Mama that if it wasn't Mack, I could keep him. But he sure didn't know what to say now that he had found that it was Mack and that the Cowarts didn't want him.

Daddy sighed at last. "Well, if you're sure. . . ."

"I don't have no way of keeping up with a dog," Mrs. Cowart said. "With Junior gone, I have to work, take care of my baby, and try to keep the farm going. I hate to keep a dog tied."

Daddy reached into his overalls pocket. He took out his wallet. "It's a hard thing, to tie a dog," he agreed. "Let me pay you for him."

"Lord," Mrs. Cowart declared, "you don't have to do that. He's been gone over six weeks, and I ain't missed him much."

But Daddy was counting out some one-dollar bills. "Five dollars?" he asked her.

Mrs. Cowart smiled and touched her fingers to her lips. "I could get my baby a little coat," she said softly. "I wanted to get her one for Christmas, but I didn't have the money."

Daddy handed the dollar bills to her. He put his hat back on. "Thank you, ma'am," he said. "I reckon the dog is kind of a Christmas present for my boy Maury here."

"How is Ben?" Mrs. Cowart said as she put the money in the pocket of her housedress. "Junior thought a lot of him. They were good friends."

"Ben's in training," Daddy explained. "He finished his basic, and now he's in a replacement training camp."

"When he finishes that, they'll send him overseas," Mrs. Cowart said. "Well, maybe the war will be over before then."

"We'll hope so," Daddy replied. "And we all hope Junior gets to come home right soon too. Good day, ma'am." He looked at me and said, "Come on, Maury. Bring your dog."

"Yes, sir!" I almost flew back to the truck.

We rattled along the dirt road for a few minutes. Daddy said, "Son, you'll have to keep the dog away from me. I don't have any use for him."

"I will, Daddy."

He sighed. "I reckon I must be next door to crazy,"

he muttered. "Wasting all this gas. Paying for a dog I'll have to feed."

"Sir, you can have the ten dollars I got for my bike. And I'll try to do chores for people to earn some money. I'll help pay for Mack's food."

"Maybe it's good for you to have a dog," Daddy said. "You're going to be a man one day, and a man has to take care of the things he loves. He's got to be responsible."

"Yes, sir," I said.

"Just keep him out of my way."

Mack was warm beside me. I think he liked the ride. He stared through the windshield, swaying as we rattled along.

After a while, Daddy almost whispered, "Maury, look at the woods."

We were passing a forest thick with dark green pines. I stared at the trees. "What is it?" I asked.

"Keep watching," Daddy said. "You'll see." He slowed the truck down.

I stared until my eyes ached. I just saw the pines. Then something swirled close to the truck. Something white.

Mack shifted next to me. I leaned close to the window and saw the whirling white specks again. "It's snowing," I said.

"Sure is," Daddy said. "We better get home before the road gets covered up." His wrinkled face wasn't smiling, but his voice sounded happier than it had since Ben had left. I put my arm over Mack's shoulders.

By the time we got to Guthrie, it was snowing pretty hard. The flakes were starting to stick to the cars parked on the square. By the time we got to Fox Road, the grass was white. And when Daddy parked the truck in front of the house, Sissy and Mama were outside. Sissy had made a little bitty snowman, no bigger than one of the cats. It was a lumpy thing, with two twigs for arms and a couple of buttons for eyes. The eyes were so big, they made it look like a snow ghost. When I opened the door of the truck and Mack jumped down, Sissy clapped her hands and squealed.

Mama smiled and dabbed at her eyes with a tissue. "This wind is making my nose run," she said. "Come on inside, you two."

By afternoon it had snowed three inches. That's a lot for Georgia. We watched the cats walking through it. Pumpkin would take a step, shake a paw, take another step, and shake that paw. He looked mad at the world for turning cold and white. When we let Mack out, he acted as though the snow were just for him. He ran and jumped, rolled over, and stuck his nose into the snow. He took a deep sniff and sneezed. I didn't have a regular sled, but Old Pa had drilled some holes in a board, put two runners on the bottom, and pulled a rope through for a handle. When I slid down the hill from the barn, Mack raced me.

After supper that night Old Pa shelled some popcorn and popped it over the fire. We sang "Jingle Bells." Daddy didn't say much. He didn't join in the song or even look at Mack. But I think Mack knew that he was home to stay. And I think he knew that Daddy was the one who had made it happen.

Chapter 7

The rest of the Christmas break flew by. Before I knew it, school had started again. Every morning Mack and I walked to the bus stop. Every afternoon he was right there under the sycamore tree waiting for me. One weekend Old Pa went rabbit hunting with Mack. He said I could come along if I stayed behind him.

We were up on the edge of the woods when Mack jumped a rabbit. I saw him freeze. He lifted one paw from the ground. His ears twitched. Old Pa watched Mack. Then he said softly, "Get him, Mack!"

Mack leaped forward. The rabbit sprang out from

the brush, and Old Pa lifted his shotgun and fired. The rabbit fell over. Mack flinched when he heard the gun. Old Pa said, "Get the rabbit, Maury. We'll have to train Mack how to bring them in before we trust him."

We got two rabbits. Old Pa dressed them, and that evening we had fried rabbit for supper. I don't reckon there's anything much tastier.

At the dinner table Old Pa said, "John, that Mack could be a good hunting dog."

"I ain't got time to train him," Daddy said.

"That's all right," Old Pa answered. He winked at me. "I reckon Maury and me can take care of that."

Well, if my life had been just weekends, training Mack to bring in a rabbit or a squirrel without biting it, I would have been happy. But school turned out to be hard work. For some reason, Miss Wilson started in on me almost as soon as school began. She was young for a teacher, with big round glasses and the greenest eyes I ever saw. She could be short-tempered too. I knew why. Miss Wilson had to tend to thirty-five young'uns in the fourth grade, and some of them would have upset an angel.

But one January afternoon, when everybody was supposed to be reading silently, she asked me to come up to her desk. She handed me a book called

David Copperfield. "I'd like you to read the first part of this out loud, Maury," she said. "Not to the class. Just to me."

Was I in trouble? I opened the book. "Chapter One," I read out loud. "I Am Born." That struck me as kind of funny. I couldn't remember a thing about being born, myself. David Copperfield told the story of his birth, though. I had read maybe four or five pages when Miss Wilson stopped me.

"Do you understand that?" she asked.

"Yes'm. I think so," I replied.

Her eyes looked huge behind her glasses. "Who's the story about?" she questioned.

"David Copperfield," I said.

"And what did you find out about David Copperfield?"

I thought for a second. "Well, ma'am, his daddy died before he was born. And his mama was pretty but sort of sickly. He had this aunt named Betsy Trotwood, who came to see him get born. Aunt Betsy wanted him to be a girl, though, so she yelled at the doctor."

"Who was Peggoty?" Miss Wilson asked.

"She worked on the place," I said. "I reckon kind of a hired hand, but a woman."

"All right," Miss Wilson said. "Go sit back down."

Well, the next day Adam Albright was calling me a teacher's pet. He kept picking at me until I couldn't hardly stand it. Being nearly a year older than the other fourth graders, I was bigger than most of them. But Adam was big too. He was a chunky kid with a tough, freckled face. And I knew he got away with stuff I'd get yelled at for doing—smoking rabbit tobacco in corncob pipes, playing hooky, and just plain meanness. Maybe he thought he had something to prove. My reading to Miss Wilson seemed to itch him somehow.

He kept pestering me at recess. "Whatcha gonna read today, Mau-ry?"

I didn't answer him. Adam wanted a fight, but he wanted me to start it. That way I'd get most of the blame and get into the most trouble. It wouldn't matter who lost or won.

He kept at me. Finally, when we were almost ready to go back inside, Adam sneered, "Your brother run off, didn't he?"

"You be quiet about my brother," I told him.

Adam grinned. He had brown teeth, what teeth he had. "Your no-good brother Ben run off," he taunted. "My pa says he had to, 'cause the sheriff was after him."

"Was not," I said.

"Was too!" Adam challenged. He poked me in the shoulder with his finger. "Your old brother wasn't nothing but a worthless peckerwood hillbilly—"

I don't even remember hitting him. One minute he was in front of me, grinning and poking at me with his finger, and the next he lay on the ground, holding his stomach.

A whistle blew. It was Mr. Garmon, who taught seventh grade and coached football and baseball. He came running over. "Break it up, boys," he said.

But there was nothing to break up. My punch had taken the wind out of Adam. He got to his feet, gasping. Fat tears rolled down his freckly face. I felt bad then. Bad, and mad at myself for letting him make me do that.

We both were sent to the principal, and we had to shake hands. When I returned to Miss Wilson's class, she told me I had to stay after school. I looked down at my feet, miserable. I was going to miss the bus, and it would take me an hour and a half to walk home. Then I'd be in worse trouble. "Yes'm," I said.

After school I waited at my desk as everyone else went out to the bus. "Well, Maury . . .," Miss Wilson started.

"I'm sorry, ma'am," I murmured. "I shouldn't have

hit him. He was saying mean things about my brother."

"Boys don't always get along with each other," she said. "But that isn't why I told you to stay. There's something I have to ask you, and then I'll drive you home." She pulled up a chair and sat down on it, next to my desk. "Maury, how would you like to go into sixth grade next year?"

"What?" I asked. I had expected to be scolded.

Miss Wilson smiled. "How would you like to skip a grade?"

I wondered how it would feel to be in a grade where people were my size. I could be in the same class as Jimmy Marshall and Frankie Carter. Miss Wilson was still waiting for my answer. I squeaked, "Could I? Skip a grade, I mean?"

"Dr. Varney thinks you could," she said. "He talked to the principal about you. The principal arranged for you to try. Would you like to do it?"

"What would I have to do?" I asked.

She looked serious. "Well, between now and June, you'd have to work extra hard. You'd have more homework and more reading. Then in June you'd take a three-hour test. If you do well enough on it, you can go into the sixth grade."

I knew spring was a busy time on the farm. With

Ben away, I had to do more work. Still, being in the sixth grade meant a lot. I thought of Mack and how hard he worked when Old Pa was teaching him to hunt. If Mack could stand it, I could. "Yes'm," I said. "I'd like that."

"Then it's a deal," she said. She held out her hand.

For a minute I didn't know what she wanted. Then I reached out and shook her hand. It made me feel funny. Kind of grown up and happy, I reckon, but kind of sad too. I don't know why.

Chapter 8

There were times that spring when I felt like quitting. Plowing time was the worst. We couldn't use the tractor because of gas rationing, so Old Pa hitched up the mules, Thunder and Lightning. All the Painter men took turns.

I don't think there's anything more tiresome than plowing. You have to lean back against the reins and keep a good hold on the plow. You have to keep your head up and make sure the mule walks a straight line. The plow blade has to cut the soil just right—not so deep it catches, not so shallow the furrow is no good. And after you do one furrow, you have to turn around and do a thousand more. Back and forth, in the hot sun, hour after hour.

Pretty soon the sweat pours down your chest, tickling like bugs crawling on you. The old mule just keeps walking, and so do you. Your view never changes. The hind end of a mule never is pretty, but after an hour of plowing, you don't want to look at another one ever again.

Mack came along on the days when I had to plow. He wanted to help. He walked beside the mule—usually Thunder, because Lightning was a mean devil who would quit on me. If Thunder started to swerve, Mack would bark. The mule would behave. When Thunder was stubborn and wanted to quit, Mack barked until he started again.

I talked to Mack. I told him about Ben and my extra lessons.

Miss Wilson had me reading a play called *Julius Caesar*, by Mr. William Shakespeare. It was tough going. Once in a while, though, I had to nod or laugh. When Julius Caesar said he didn't like men with "a lean and hungry look," but wanted men about him who were "fat, sleek-headed," it made me laugh out loud. I couldn't help but remember the man who had made a speech on the Guthrie square one time. Daddy said he was running for governor.

He was fat and sleek, all right. Old Julius would've purely liked *him*.

Anyhow, parts of that play caught in my memory, like logs floating down a river. They stuck somehow. One hot Saturday morning, halfway through an acre of plowing, a speech from the play came to me. "Friends, Romans, countrymen," I said, "lend me your ears. I come to bury Caesar, not to praise him." Well, I wasn't talking to any friends or Romans, but to a dog and the hind end of a mule. Mack looked interested, though. I talked my way all through that speech, then asked Mack, "How did I remember all that, do you reckon?"

Mack sat down on a furrow and scratched his ear. He didn't know. He didn't even know how he'd learned to have such a soft mouth that he could fetch rabbit without ruffling a hair on its body. Hunting just came naturally to Mack. Somehow book learning came naturally to me.

Before I knew it, it was April and Easter time. We never had much cash in the house, but somehow every Easter Mama found enough to get Sissy and me some clothes and shoes. About a week before Easter, she took us into town. Guthrie had one big store, the Gallant-Belk. I liked watching the clerks send orders and money whizzing through tubes powered by air. The store had a special odor too. Everything smelled new.

Mama always insisted that we walk around some in new shoes. She said that one thing that standing up all day being a teacher had taught *her* was that unhappy feet make an unhappy person. Mama bought me a pair of black oxfords. Sissy got some patent-leather shoes. Mama said to me, "I suppose you're old enough to wear long pants this Easter." She bought a pair of dark brown pants, a white shirt, and a clip-on tie. It was the first tie I'd ever owned.

Then Sissy had to try on about a million dresses. She wound up with a frilly pink one. When we got out of the store, Old Pa, who had driven us into town in the wagon, was sitting on one of the benches in the town square. Mack lay on the grass beside him. Old Pa was talking to four other men. One of them said, "That there's a likely looking bird dog, Maury. You want to sell him?"

"No, sir," I declared.

The man grinned all over his wrinkly face. "Don't blame you one bit," he said, and the other men laughed.

We got back in the wagon and rumbled out of

town. "Next fall, we'll try Mack out on quail," Old Pa said. "I think he'll be a first-rate bird dog."

I didn't say anything. More and more, I was getting not to like hunting so much. Not that I'd ever stop eating the rabbits or squirrels that Daddy and Old Pa brought home. I just didn't like shooting them myself. That was strange, because when the weather turned cold, I helped at hog butchering. Somehow I felt different about killing the littler animals, though.

Fishing, on the other hand, didn't bother me a bit. I could take a pole and line to Walnut Creek, which ran along the back of our property, and bring home a mess of panfish. Once in a while, I'd get as far as Tully's Lake and catch a bass or two. I'd dig in when Mama cooked them, proud I'd put food on our table.

"Maury, how are your studies coming along?" Mama asked, interrupting my daydream.

I shrugged. "Reading is easy," I said. "Arithmetic is hard."

"I'll help you with it," she said.

It was true, what I told her. I enjoyed reading, even when I had to stop and look up every other word. Adding and subtracting were all right, and

I knew my times tables up to twelve times twelve. But the devil himself must have invented long division.

Sissy said, "I want to bring my dolly to church in a new Easter dress."

Mama put her hand on Sissy's hair and smoothed it. "I think your dolly better stay home," she said.

"But I want the preacher to see her," Sissy insisted.

Mama smiled. "Reverend Thompson will see her next Sunday. He's going to have dinner with us."

I groaned. Jimmy Marshall had told me that Mr. Leroy Scoggins, the Baptist preacher, was a big eater. We were Methodists, but I reckon Reverend Thompson could give any Baptist a run for his money. When Reverend Thompson ate with us, he ate and ate and ate until I wondered where he put it all. And he ate the best parts too. If we had rabbit, he got the tender saddle. If we had chicken, he got the pulley bone. Mama always made a big Easter dinner, but if the preacher was eating with us, there wouldn't be much left over.

When we got home, Sissy went to feed the hens. All of our chickens except Miss Priss and her family were white leghorns. Sissy had named the black speckly hen "Miss Priss" because she stayed apart from the other chickens. Miss Priss now had a brood of six half-grown speckly pullets. They weren't chicks anymore, but they came running and peeping when Sissy scattered the food.

It was Saturday, so I changed into my oldest clothes and helped Daddy plant. We had a hundred and twenty acres in cotton, forty acres in corn, a few acres in sugarcane, and our garden patch.

I hated cotton. First you had to plow. Next you had to plant. Then you had to chop the weeds all summer through. And at the end of the summer, you had to sling a bag over your shoulder and, sunup to sundown, you stooped along, picking the fluffy cotton out of the dried bolls.

The bolls split open and the sharp stickers on the end pricked your fingers. A boll of cotton didn't weigh anything. Nor did it take up much room. You'd pick and pick for hours, and still just the bottom of your sack would be full. I despised cotton, from planting to the time we plowed the old plants under.

That evening, I took Mack to Walnut Creek. I had my fishing pole along. In the woods I found some rotten logs with grubs inside. They're kind of squooshy and disgusting, but they make good bait.

Mack lay on the bank while I fished. After four

months he looked a whole lot better than when I'd found him. His fur was glossy and shiny. His ribs no longer stood out. And I liked the way his brown eyes shone.

He got real excited when I caught a fish. It was a good-sized bream, so I strung it and left it in a pool. Mack guarded the string while I caught another one and then another. I had to laugh at the way he watched me pull the fish from the water. He tilted his head as if he were memorizing what I was doing in case he ever wanted to fish himself.

When I started home about sundown, Mack ran alongside me. As we went past the barn, Mack rushed ahead. I think he knew I was bringing supper home, and he wanted to tell everybody. But he saw Daddy in the yard, and he stopped running. Slowly he came back to me.

Daddy never spoke a kind word to Mack. He didn't treat the dog badly, but he never seemed to notice him. Mack seemed to want to stay out of Daddy's way too. He walked behind me as I got close to the house.

Daddy looked up. "Pretty good string," he said.

"Yes, sir."

"Well, clean 'em and I'll tell Mama we're having fish for supper."

I took the fish out back of the house. Pumpkin and Squirrel showed up. The two cats begged for the fish heads. Mack didn't bother them. He just sat down and looked at the two cats as if he thought they were crazy.

When I finished, Mama fried up the fish. I was happy. Easter was just a week away. Seemed to me like nothing was going to trouble us. I was wrong.

Chapter 9

Easter Sunday came. We sat in the middle of Hopewell Methodist Church and listened to Reverend Thompson talk about Jesus. The Reverend wasn't rightly a fat man, but he was big. He was a lot wider than Daddy, and not as tall.

After the service the preacher stood at the door shaking hands. He said he would see us along about two o'clock for dinner. Mama told him we were having fried chicken, and that man's eyes lit up. He reminded me of a jack-o'-lantern at Halloween.

At home Mama got us all busy. Mack was used to playing with me when I came home from church.

He stood on the front porch peering in through the screen. He kept whining. He wanted to run and play, and he didn't understand why I was cooped up inside. I was tidying up the front room, though it wasn't really dirty.

All the while, delicious smells came from the kitchen. Mama had Sissy peel some potatoes. I could smell the chicken frying. It was going to be a great big double batch. Mama was making buttermilk biscuits and cooking some of the green beans she had canned last summer. I got hungrier and hungrier.

Sissy and I set the table. First we put on the red-and-white checked tablecloth that was for special times like Christmas, or when we had company. Then we put out the Blue Willow china and the good glasses. About the time we finished setting the table, the preacher came rolling up in his car. Daddy and Old Pa and he sat on the front porch while Mama, Sissy, and I put the food out.

Then Mama sent me to call them in. I got to the front door and heard Daddy saying, "No, Ben's about finished with his training. Then he'll go off to fight. I hope he goes to Europe and not the Pacific."

"We'll remember him in prayer," the preacher said.

I felt awfully funny hearing Daddy speak about Ben. Ben wrote a letter home every week, and I knew

Mama wrote to him. Daddy never read the letters, though. Mama would tell me some of the things that Ben said, but never when Daddy was in the room. Did she talk to Daddy about Ben when I wasn't around?

I called everyone in to dinner. Mack wanted to come too, but Old Pa kept him out. It wasn't fitting to let a dog eat in the same room as a preacher, I supposed.

We all sat down at the table. Mama put out the biggest platter of fried chicken I had ever seen in my life. That chicken was brown and perfect. It just *glowed.* My mouth started to water. I knew how tender Mama's fried chicken was. It simply melted in your mouth.

Reverend Thompson said, "May we pray?" We bowed our heads, and he said what felt like the longest grace that anybody had ever said in the entire history of Christianity. It was pure torture, with that smell in my nose. My stomach growled three times.

Finally he said "Amen," and we started to pass the chicken around. Sure enough, he took two pulley bones. I took a drumstick, and Sissy got one too.

"These ought to be good chickens," Old Pa said. "We killed the two fattest hens for this meal."

"They smell delicious," Reverend Thompson said.

"Yep," Old Pa said. "One of them was a young white leghorn, and the other was a speckly hen."

"What?" Sissy said.

Daddy looked at her. "Hush," he said.

Sissy stood up. Her chin was just a little higher than the table. "What did Old Pa say?"

Daddy sighed. "Sit back down, hon. Old Pa said one of these chickens was a white leghorn, and the other was that black speckled one."

Sissy stared at her plate. Her lip trembled. "Miss Priss?" she asked. "You killed *Miss Priss?*"

"It was just a chicken," Daddy said.

Sissy gulped some deep breaths. "Miss Priss wanted to live," she said. "Same as us."

Preacher Thompson had one of those pulley bones about halfway to his mouth. He stared at it. I looked at the drumstick on my own plate.

"Now, Sissy," Daddy said.

Sissy pushed her plate away. "I don't want to eat Miss Priss," she bawled. Tears were running down her cheeks.

"It's good," Old Pa told her. "You know how you love your mama's chicken."

Sissy buried her head in her hands and sobbed

like her heart had been broken. I pushed my plate back too. I was remembering how I felt about shooting rabbits and squirrels.

Mama said softly, "Maybe I'll just have vegetables."

Daddy said, "Well, I'm going to have chicken!" He got himself a thigh.

Sissy watched him. Her face was scrunched up. Daddy started to take a bite. "Poor Miss Priss," Sissy said.

Daddy put the thigh down.

Reverend Thompson put the pulley bone down. Old Pa sighed. "Well, what are we going to do?"

Daddy got up. He went out of the room, and when he came back, he had a big cardboard boot box in his hand. "Give me your chicken," he said to me.

He put every last piece of chicken in that boot box. Then he said, "Come on. Bring the box, Maury."

We went out to the yard. Mack smelled the chicken and got real excited. The cats came. Daddy got a shovel from the shed and started to dig. He dug a deep hole.

"Now," he said. "Maury, put the box in there."

The cardboard was getting spotty with grease. I

put it down into the hole. Daddy shoveled dirt over it and told me to get some rocks from the pile near the henhouse.

I lugged five big flat river rocks over. Daddy covered the fried chicken grave with them so that Mack couldn't dig up the box. "There," he said.

Reverend Thompson looked right puzzled. "I suppose I should say a word," he said.

"Bow your heads," Daddy said.

The preacher said a few words about hens. He said they were God's creatures and the life of a hen could mean as much to some people as the life of anything else. He said he hoped God would bless us all.

"Well," Daddy said when the preacher had finished. "We gave Miss Priss a good funeral. Do you feel better?"

Sissy nodded, all smiles again. "Can I put some flowers here?" she asked.

"Put all the flowers you want," Daddy said.

Well, the vegetables were good, anyway. I thought that ended it. But along about the next Wednesday, I saw that something new had been added. Old Pa had whittled out a marker for that fried chicken grave. It was a sitting hen, looking just like Miss Priss, feathers and all. And on it he had carved, "To the Memory of Miss Priss and the Unknown Hen."

Sissy had put a jar with fresh flowers on that little grave. Every week she would kneel and take the old flowers and replace them with new ones. Mack would go with her. He looked so mournful you might have thought he was related to that chicken. Sissy said he missed his little friend.

Personally I believe that what Mack missed was a great fried chicken dinner.

Chapter 10

Somehow or other the weeks rolled by. When I had time between hoeing and studying and milking the cows and feeding the pigs, I played with Mack. He loved to fetch. I had a beat-up old baseball that I would throw for him. He'd bound after it, ears flying and tongue flapping. That dog never got tired.

I sure did, though. Miss Wilson said that she was right proud of me, that since January, I'd finished all my fourth-grade work and about all the fifth-grade work too. Mrs. Gould, the librarian, gave me a certificate one day. I had checked out and read more books than anybody in school. She smiled at me so widely that I could see the gold hooks that kept her false teeth in place.

At home, Mama kept after me on the arithmetic. Finally I got long division through my head. As May passed by, I felt more and more as though I'd been running without taking a breath. I started looking forward to summer.

We got a letter from Ben one day. He was overseas. He said all he could tell us was that he was in England. Sissy and I found England in my geography book. She said it looked like a little bitty place. I told her it was little, and it was old. She listened to me talk about knights in armor and kings and queens and old William Shakespeare. She liked the part about the queens.

Mostly, though, as the days got hot, I just looked ahead to summer. Along about the end of May, Miss Wilson told me that Tuesday, June 13, was going to be an important day. School would be out by then, but on that day the principal would give me the test so I could be promoted to the sixth grade.

Mama marked the date on our calendar. I began to get nervous. My head was stuffed so full that I was afraid things might get stuck in there. What if I tried to take the test and couldn't think of a thing? Mama told me not to worry.

One morning at the end of May, Mrs. Gould asked me to help her move some books in the library. I noticed a bunch of old books piled in a trash can near the library door. "What are these, ma'am?" I asked.

Mrs. Gould was a gray-haired lady with eyes as sharp as two pins. "Those are books we are discarding," she said. "They're old and past repair."

Well, all the time we toted books, that pile in the trash kept drawing my attention. When we took a rest, I reached into the trash can and dug two books out. My heart beat fast. "Ma'am? If it's all the same to you, could I have some of these?"

Mrs. Gould gave me a puzzled look. "An old copy of *The Complete Works of Shakespeare*, Volume One and Volume Three? Maury, half that set is missing."

"Yes, ma'am, but the part that's here is good."

A long time before, Mrs. Gould had put up a war poster on the library wall. It said, "Use it up, wear it out, make it do, or do without," reminding people that the war meant we had to save every little thing. She looked at the poster and gave me her gold-edged smile. "You're welcome to as many old books as you want."

I took half of the complete works of Shakespeare, some Sherlock Holmes stories, *Pilgrim's Progress*, and most of *Robinson Crusoe*. There was a *Treasure Island* that someone had drawn pirates and parrots in and a book called *Apiculture* that was about bees, not apes, and pretty dull.

Old Pa put a shelf over my bed for my collection. Daddy had told me many times that farmers didn't need a library, but I loved having my own books.

School finally ended. That June was fine and hot. The corn rose high and green, with that sweet growing smell nothing but corn has. At night, lightning bugs winked their yellow lights all across the pasture.

Work didn't end when school ended. Daddy was busy with the cotton crop. He put me in charge of our vegetable patch, which was coming along well. Lots of times in the past few years raccoons had raided our garden. This year, though, Mack scared them away. Nothing is cuter than a little raccoon, with his bandit mask and big eyes. But one or two of those rascals can purely ruin a garden.

One hot Tuesday evening, I was hoeing in the vegetable patch. I had finished with the beans and the squash and had just started chopping the weeds from around the tomato plants, which were big and full. Some of the heavy green tomatoes were already turning pink.

Suddenly Sissy appeared. "Maury!" she yelled. "Maury, you come quick! Mama's crying!"

I dropped the hoe and ran all the way to the house. I was barefooted and stubbed my toe on a tree root, hard enough to make me whistle, but I never stopped. Mack was in the yard jumping around. He rushed to join me.

We banged through the kitchen door. "Mama?" I called. The radio was playing in the front room. A man was talking in an excited voice. I hurried in there, with Mack's toenails clicking right behind me. Mama was sitting in the armchair. She had her hand over her eyes. "What is it, Mama?"

The man on the radio said, "D day, the sixth of June." He explained how the American and English armies had invaded France and how lots of men had been killed or wounded. Mama's eyes were red. "Ben's there," she whispered. "They invaded from England. His infantry division is in the heaviest fighting."

I sank down on the floor. The radio was a big old thing with a lighted yellow dial and about a dozen knobs. You could get shortwave stations and regular stations. I listened as hard as I could.

The Germans had conquered France about four

years earlier. Now the English and the Americans were trying to take France back from Germany. The reporter on the radio was at the front and the booming of the big guns and the roaring of the airplanes could be heard in the background. I closed my eyes and imagined what it would be like to shoot at people and be shot at by them. I tried to picture my brother Ben fighting, but couldn't do it.

All that week Mama listened to the war news. The American army drove deeper and deeper into France. The fighting was hard. Daddy didn't listen to the news, but he didn't tell us we couldn't.

We didn't hear from Ben, or even know exactly where he was, until Monday, the twelfth of June. That was the day before I was supposed to take my test to skip the fifth grade.

With worrying about Ben and the test, I could hardly sleep. That Monday morning, Mama served breakfast, but none of us had much appetite. After breakfast, Mama asked me to chop some firewood for the stove. That's where I was when Mack began barking. I rushed to the house to see what was the matter. Mama stood on the front porch.

A car had stopped in front of the house. Two men got out. One of them was Reverend Thompson, looking solemn. The other was a lieutenant in the army. They came slowly down the front walk. Both of them took off their hats.

Mama didn't turn to look at me, but she knew I was there. "It's Ben," she said. "Maury, go get your father."

I ran with Mack bounding right beside me. He thought it was a race. We dashed through the pasture and up to the cornfield. Daddy was there with a hoe in his hand. I yelled for him. He looked around, sharp. "What is it?" he hollered.

"Ben!" I screamed. "Something about Ben!"

Daddy dropped his hoe and came running. He passed me, easy. I followed, already out of breath. Mack hung back and stayed with me.

When I got to the house, the preacher and the army lieutenant were driving off. Daddy stood on the porch, his arm around Mama's waist. "What is it?" I asked Daddy. He shook his head and went inside. Mama was crying.

Old Pa came out of the house and put his hand on my shoulder. He handed me a telegram. It began, THE SECRETARY OF THE ARMY REGRETS TO INFORM YOU THAT YOUR SON, PFC BENJAMIN F. PAINTER, IS MISSING IN ACTION.

I couldn't read more than that.

"What does this mean?" I asked Old Pa.

Old Pa cleared his throat. "Your brother was in the fight over in France. He got separated from his outfit somehow. They don't know where he is. He might be wounded."

Sissy was swinging on the screen door. She loved to do that, though Daddy scolded her. "Ben could be dead," she said. She was crying without sobbing. Tears poured off her face.

I looked up at Old Pa. He nodded and whispered, "Yes, Ben could be dead."

I glared at Sissy. "You get off that door right now!" I yelled. Then she began to cry out loud. She jumped off the door and ran around in back of the house.

"Maury," Old Pa said.

I turned and screamed, "He ain't dead! He ain't!" Then I ran off too—all the way to Walnut Creek. I threw myself down on the bank and cried. By and by Mack lay down beside me. He didn't whimper, and he didn't lick my face. He was just there. I put my arm over him. My brother's dog.

That evening we walked slowly back to the house. Dinner was awfully quiet. Mama asked me to help her wash dishes after we had finished eating. While I was drying the plates, she said, "You ought to go to bed early, Maury. You've got a big day tomorrow."

A lump swelled up in my throat. "Mama, I can't take that test."

"You most certainly can." Mama pushed a strand of hair out of her eyes. "You can take it, and you will."

It was hard not to cry. "I can't even think of arithmetic and English, Mama. With Ben—it just—"

"Sit down, Maury," Mama said.

We sat at the dinner table, and she took both of my hands in hers. For a little while we sat like that. Her hands were small, but they weren't soft. Working on the farm had made them tough, almost leathery. Finally she said, "You mean to tell me you're going to give up now? You didn't give up when you wanted Mack to stay, did you? You didn't let anything stop you."

"No'm," I mumbled.

"I'll tell you something else, Maury," Mama said. "I wrote to Ben and told him about your chance to skip a grade. Do you want to know what he thought about that?" She reached into the big pocket in her apron and pulled out a thin paper, the kind that Ben wrote his letters on. It folded so that the letter made its own envelope. She unfolded it and put it on the table.

Mack, who had been sitting in the corner, came over and sat next to me as I read my brother's round handwriting. Ben never could spell *cat*, but that didn't matter to me. Ben had written, "Well I gess Maury has a great chance now. I no he will do good on the test. You tell him for me that he is the smart one in the famly and I am prowd of him."

"You see?" Mama asked, smoothing my hair. "You're not taking this test just for yourself, Maury. You're doing it for Ben, for me, for Old Pa, for Sissy, and for your father."

My breath came in a long, shaky sigh. "All right," I said. "I'll try."

Mack put his paw on my knee, as if saying, "That's all you have to do."

If only it would be enough.

Chapter 11

The next morning Old Pa hitched up the mules, and we went to the school. Mack rode along with us. Old Pa said he and Mack would ramble around in the woods behind the school until the test was over, and he sent me on in.

The principal wasn't there, but Miss Deaton, the school secretary, was. She took me to the library and put the test papers on a table. "You'll have until twelve o'clock, Maury," she said. "Good luck."

I was sitting beside an open window and could see the playground and the woods beyond. Old Pa and Mack walked slowly away. Old Pa looked bent and sad. Mack walked with his head low, as if he felt Old Pa's sorrow.

They disappeared into the woods, and I picked up my pencil. The first part of the test was English, and it was pretty easy. Drawing diagrams of sentences was the hardest part, but there wasn't much of that. Then the math questions started. The word problems made my head spin. One train left Chicago at seven in the morning going toward New York at fifty miles an hour, and another one left New York at nine o'clock heading toward Chicago at sixty miles per hour. Why didn't folks just stay home?

The math was so hard that it nearly drove geography out of my head, and that was the last part of the test. When I finished the geography, I went back and puzzled over the math for a few minutes more, until Miss Deaton came to take the test away.

"How'd you do?" Old Pa asked when I climbed into the wagon.

I put my arm around Mack. His black coat was hot from the sun, and he leaned comfortably against me. "I don't know," I said. It was the truth. That test made me feel as if my head had emptied. Old Pa clucked to the mules, and the wagon rumbled away toward home.

Mama was hanging out wash when we got back.

"How did you do?" she asked me.

"I tried my best," I said.

That day and the days that followed felt strange, like time in a dream. Mama did everything as always, cooking and cleaning and taking care of the chores. She was different, though. She would sit in her rocker on the front porch, her hands folded on her lap, staring across the road at the cotton field. Her lips didn't move, and she didn't make a sound, but I knew she was praying for Ben at those times.

We all prayed for him. At night I dreamed about Ben. In those dreams he was tall and laughing. Sometimes he was home and went hunting with Mack, and from the woods came the sound of gunfire. But it was the big guns, the cannons. That always made me wake up, scared.

Lots of times in those long nights I would sit up in bed and pet Mack. He was supposed to sleep outdoors, but ever since the telegram came, I had let him stay in my bedroom. It was a comfort to have him curled up at the foot of my bed.

The worst nights were the ones when I woke up and heard a soft, distant sound, one that reminded me of the sad song of the mourning doves. Mama was crying again. She never let us see her crying, but she did it almost every night. If I'd thought moving the earth would make her stop, I would have tried to do it.

Daddy never talked to me about Ben. Through those June weeks he had me beside him in the fields. We did just about everything together, from chopping weeds in the cotton field to picking beans and mending some loose boards in the barn where Lightning had kicked the walls. Daddy spoke just enough to get me to hand him some nails or clean out the cow stalls. That was all.

One evening about two weeks after the telegram had come, I sat on the front porch with Mama. She was in her chair, rocking slowly. I sat on the edge of the porch, with my feet on the top step. Across the cotton fields lightning bugs blinked on and off, hundreds of them. Mack lay on the porch behind me, and I leaned back into him. He was like a soft cushion, his breathing regular and calm.

"I wish we would hear from Ben," I said softly.

"Maury," Mama said.

"Ben can't be dead, Mama," I told her. "If he was, we'd know. Somehow we'd know." When she didn't say anything, I added, "If we had word from Ben, maybe Daddy would feel better. He won't talk or anything. He acts like it's his fault that Ben is missing."

"Your father's sad because he and Ben never made up after their quarrel," Mama whispered. "That's what bothers him."

"He doesn't act sad," I had to say. "He acts like he's mad at me. At the whole world. Why does Daddy have to be so mad all the time?"

"Maury," Mama said again. Then she started to cry.

I got up and stood beside her. "I'm sorry, Mama."

She squeezed my hand. "Life can be hard sometimes, Maury. We have to deal with it. We have to do our best, that's all. I hope Ben is alive somewhere. Every day I pray to hear word of him. But if he's gone, then we have to accept that. It's the way life can be. We'll never forget Ben, though—" She broke down then.

That made me feel awful. I didn't mean to cause her pain. That night I couldn't sleep. Crickets chirped outside, and somewhere an owl hooted mournfully, over and over.

Mack stirred at the foot of my bed. He came up to lick my face. I turned over, and he poked me with his nose. "What is it?" I asked him.

Mack whined a little.

"You need to go out?" I said.

He whined again.

I got out of bed and pulled my overalls on. I went downstairs barefooted in the dark. The old floorboards were rough under my feet, and some of them squeaked. As we walked through the kitchen, I heard the clock in the front room strike three low *bongs*. Three o'clock in the morning.

I opened the back door. The moon wasn't all the way full, but it shone bright, a pale half-closed eye in the dark face of night. The backyard was all silver with moonlight.

I expected Mack to do his business and then come back in. Instead he walked to the side of the house. He gave me a long look. Then he hurried around to the front.

What in the world was wrong with him? I went through the kitchen and into the front room. The door stood open. Through the screen I could see the porch.

Daddy was sitting on the edge of the porch with his feet on the steps, just the way I had been sitting six hours earlier. He seemed so lonesome and sad that it made me catch my breath.

Mack came around the corner of the house and paused at the bottom of the steps. He gazed up at

Daddy. I thought he was remembering how Daddy always grumbled at him or pushed him away with his foot.

I didn't say a word. I couldn't. Daddy's back was to me, so he didn't see me.

Mack slowly walked up the steps and sat down next to Daddy.

Daddy raised his head and looked at Mack. He put his arms around Mack. Mack leaned close to him and tried to lick his face. Then Daddy buried his face in Mack's shoulder. I could hear Daddy crying. It was the first time I had ever heard that.

I went back upstairs alone. I lay down in the dark, and felt worse than I had ever felt before. For the first time it seemed to me that Ben was never going to come home again.

Chapter 12

On July 3, Daddy and I were working in the cotton field when an old Ford came rattling down the road, raising a big cloud of red dust. It was slowing down, and I straightened to stare at it. Was someone bringing us news of Ben at last?

The car rumbled into our driveway, and Daddy and I hurried to it. But Miss Wilson got out of the car, not an army man. Mama came out of the house, drying her hands on a dish towel. Sissy had been throwing a stick for Mack to chase, and the two of them came from the backyard. Old Pa was still up in the cornfield.

Miss Wilson was smiling. "Hello," she said. She shook hands with Daddy. "Mr. Painter, you have a bright son."

Mama put her hand to her mouth. She was smiling, but her eyes were bright with tears. "Oh, Maury," she said.

Miss Wilson handed me a paper. "Congratulations, Maury," she said. "You're going to be in the sixth grade."

"Thank you," I said, looking at the certificate. It had my name, and a gold seal in the corner. The principal and even the chairman of the county board of education had signed it.

Daddy put his hand on my shoulder. "I'm proud of my boy," he said.

I felt about ten feet tall. Mama asked Miss Wilson to come in and have some tea, and the two of them went inside the house. I showed the certificate to Sissy and Mack. "This is my name, right here," I explained, pointing.

Daddy patted my shoulder again. "Better put it up where it won't get dirty," he said. "We've got more weeds to hoe."

Boy, I hated cotton.

Mack and I went inside and Mama called me over to the table. It felt strange, seeing my teacher sitting in our kitchen, but Miss Wilson was smiling at me. "You did fine on the test," she said. "You had to make eighty percent to pass. Do you know what your score was?"

I shook my head.

"Ninety-two," she told me. "Maury, you can do just about anything you want. After high school, you might even go to college. You can be anything you can think of. Just work hard and keep trying."

"Yes'm."

Mama took the certificate and said she'd find a frame for it. Then Mack and I went back out, Mack to chase sticks and me to chop weeds with a hoe, trying hard not to bring it down on my foot. That would be an easy way to lose a big toe. The sun was still hot on my back. We still hadn't heard anything about Ben. Nothing much seemed to have changed.

If I were just making up a story for a book, we would have heard from Ben the next day, the Fourth of July. But we didn't. The hot days went by, and though I was happy that I had done well on the test, life still seemed unreal, like a bad dream that none of us could wake up from.

Two weeks later, on a day when Old Pa and Daddy had taken the wagon into Guthrie to sell some corn, beans, squash, and tomatoes, I was lying in the shade of an apple tree behind the house, reading a mystery. Sherlock Holmes was trying to find out if a ghostly hound dog was really killing the Baskerville family. Mack lay by my side, yawning.

We heard a funny sound. It was an engine, but not a car. A man came down the dirt road on a motor scooter, and he stopped at the house. From out front I heard Mama yell, "Maury!"

Mack and I ran. The man had climbed back onto his scooter and puttered off. Mama was on the front porch, holding a yellow Western Union envelope in her hands. She was shaking all over. "It's a telegram," she said. "Read it, Maury. I can't."

My heart felt as if it were about to burst. Telegrams meant bad news. I didn't want to read it. But I had to.

My hands were trembling. I got the thin paper out and unfolded it. The words leaped off the page at me.

```
THE SECRETARY OF THE ARMY WISHES TO
INFORM YOU THAT PFC BENJAMIN F.
PAINTER, PREVIOUSLY LISTED AS MISS-
ING IN ACTION, IS ALIVE....
```

There was more, but Mama didn't let me read it. She fell on her knees and hugged me, laughing and crying. She yelled for Sissy, and we all piled into the truck. I didn't even know Mama could drive. She never had before. She got that truck cranked, though, and we tore off for Guthrie. We stopped in front of Produce Row, where all the farmers brought their vegetables. Daddy and Old Pa were at the near end, their wagon half empty.

Daddy saw us and jumped up, but Mama was already out of the truck. She called, "Oh, John," and ran to hug Daddy. People crowded all around us, and soon they were shaking my hand and laughing. Old Pa came over and said, "You and Sissy can stay here with me. I think your mama and daddy need to be alone."

So they drove back home in the truck. We stayed and purely sold vegetables. Everybody came to our wagon, and nobody left without a few ears of corn or a few pounds of beans. Sissy took the quarters and dimes and put them in Old Pa's money bag. Everybody told us how glad they were to hear the good news.

Later we rode back to the farm in the wagon. Then I learned the news wasn't all good, when Mama told me about the rest of the telegram.

Ben wasn't dead, but he had been wounded and taken prisoner. The Germans had held him in a prison camp for weeks. Then some English soldiers had rescued him. Now he was in an English hospital.

But even so, he was alive. And before long we got a letter from him that said he would be coming home soon. That was like a light coming on in a dim room. Daddy laughed all the time. Old Pa seemed thirty years younger as he taught Mack to fetch a quail, which was much more delicate than a rabbit, without crushing it. Mama just couldn't stop smiling. Even Mack seemed glad. He walked around wagging that long pointer tail of his, and Daddy petted him whenever he passed by.

That was a long, long summer, the summer of 1944. Finally there came a late-August day when we all got into the wagon and rode to Guthrie. A Greyhound bus pulled up to the Gulf station. A tall, skinny, brown-haired soldier got out, walking slowly on crutches.

It was my brother Ben, home for good. Mama hugged and hugged him. Sissy, who said she could remember him, just stood staring at him. She acted as though she'd never seen him before. Daddy hugged him, and Old Pa did too. Ben reached out and ruffled up my hair. "You've about got grown," he said.

"I'm trying," I replied. It didn't seem possible that he had been away just one year. He was awfully thin, and his face was pinched and white. He wore ribbons on his uniform. One of them was a Purple Heart, which showed he had been wounded in action.

On the way to the farm Ben told us he had been shot in both legs. For a while he was afraid the German doctors were going to cut off his legs, but they didn't. Ben was getting a medical discharge and would soon be out of the army. He had done his part. The Purple Heart and Silver Star beside it told how brave he had been. Ben could have returned without them, though, and we'd have been just as happy.

When we got home, Old Pa and Daddy helped Ben down from the wagon. The preacher was there, and Miss Wilson, and lots of our neighbors. We were going to have a big barbecue to celebrate.

Only I didn't want to see anybody, not just then. All summer, I had felt empty. Now somehow that feeling was hard to shake, even with Ben home again. I walked up behind the barn with Mack and sat in the sun with my back against the old wood. I had one hand on Mack's neck. He panted happily.

After a while I heard someone coming. To my surprise Ben swung himself around the corner of the barn on those crutches. "Hey, hotshot," he said.

"Hey yourself," I replied. Then I said, "Your dog came back."

"Mama told me." Ben stood there watching me and Mack. "I reckon he's your dog now."

"Really?" I asked. Then I knew what had been bothering me. It was good to have Ben home again, but Mack was supposed to be Ben's dog, not mine. "I can have him?"

"Seems to me you have each other," Ben said. "Here, Mack! Come here, boy."

Mack looked at him and wagged his tail. He didn't move from my side, though.

Ben nodded. "Yep, he's your dog, sure enough." He spread the crutches out, put his back against the barn, and eased himself down to sit beside me. "You're going to have to help me get back up again. Still can't do that with these blamed crutches."

"I'll help you."

"Doctors say it's gonna take a year for me to learn to walk without them. I'm gonna fool them, though. Gonna be walking all on my own by Christmas. Promised myself that. Think I can do it, hotshot?"

I nodded. "You can do anything you want to do."

Ben took a deep breath. He picked up a handful of soil and let it trickle from his fist. "You know, when I left, I couldn't wait to get away from this red-dirt farm," he said. "And I spent almost all my time away wanting to get back here."

"I'm glad you made it back okay," I said.

"You and me both, little brother." Ben reached over to ruffle Mack's ears. Mack put up with it. But he acted as if it were a stranger touching him. He didn't try to lick Ben's face, the way he always did with me or Sissy.

"Are you going to stay here on the farm?" I asked him.

Ben nodded. "I sure am. I guess I'll ask Libby Turner if she still wants to marry me. She likes farm life, and Mama and Daddy like her. Figure we can build us a little house across the road there, at the end of the cotton field. That's where we'll spend the rest of our days. I reckon God just cut me out to be a farmer."

"Daddy will sure be glad to have you back," I said.

Ben didn't say anything for a few minutes. Then he said, "Maury, I'm going to stay on the farm. That don't mean you have to, though."

I didn't know what he meant. "I'm only ten," I told him. "Going on eleven. I'm not about to leave."

Ben laughed. "Miss Wilson's been talking to me about you. I heard about your being so smart in school. Smarter than I ever was. Maury, it's about time a Painter finished high school and went to college. You ought to be the one to do it too. How would you like that?"

"I don't know," I said. Thinking about such things made my heart beat a little faster. College was where you could read all the books you wanted. Nobody would tell you to stop reading and start plowing. You'd never have to look at a mule's rear end. Still, college was such a long way off that I couldn't imagine it. One year seemed to last almost forever. How could I even think about something that was seven or eight years away?

"Well," Ben said, "you consider it, that's all. I know it would please Mama, and you don't know how proud it would make Daddy. You're not gonna let them down, are you?"

"No, sir," I said.

He messed up my hair. "Don't you ever call me 'sir' again," he said. "I'm not an officer. I work for a living. Now I want you to come back to the house with me and eat some barbecue. Help me up."

I tugged on his arm, and together we got him to his feet. Then I walked down to the house beside my brother, where a long table under the sycamore tree was groaning with big bowls of potato salad, corn on the cob, fried green tomatoes, fried chicken, and barbecue. Everybody had lots to eat, and Mack got plenty of leftovers to keep him happy.

That evening after everyone had gone home, and Ben was in the front room telling Sissy, Old Pa, Daddy, and Mama about his adventures, I slipped outside. Mack came with me, as he always did. On the front porch I could still hear Ben's voice coming through the screen behind me. I rested my cheek on Mack's soft neck. The sun had just set, but the sky was still light, with pink clouds over in the west. Birds were singing sleepy songs. Overhead some swifts were streaking and twittering through the air, hunting for gnats and mosquitoes. The calm evening smelled warm and sweet, with a faint promise of coolness to come. For the first time in months I felt all right.

I might one day get to go to college. I might not. It didn't matter much to me right then. What did matter was that the family was back together. Ben was home, and Daddy was happy he was there, and Mama could stop crying.

Before you knew it, fall would come. Soon the leaves would turn red and yellow, and the geese would fly in high, honking vees. At school I'd be in the sixth grade with my friends. Some frosty morning Old Pa, Ben, and I would see how good a quail-hunting dog Mack had become. I knew he would be a fine one.

Then beyond fall would be Christmas, with us all together, the way we should be. And by Christmas, you could bet that stubborn Ben would surely be off those crutches. When spring came, we'd work in the fields together.

Maybe I would tell Ben some of the things I had read. There was a play by William Shakespeare that had a speech about soldiers in it. A king told his men that they would always be heroes for fighting in a battle on St. Crispin's Day.

That was a hard speech to understand. I had learned it by heart, though. Saying it out loud made me feel kind of proud and tall. I didn't know when St. Crispin's Day was, but I would always remember the sixth of June, D day, the day when my brother Ben became a hero. And he always would be.

After a while, I got up and stretched. Mack went off into the dusk and came back with his old beat-up baseball. He held it up and gave me a kind of hopeful look. I laughed and took the ball. We went to the backyard, where I spent an hour throwing that ball into the dark for my dog to fetch.

Now, if this was only a story in a book, Mack

would have saved somebody's life, maybe. He might have rescued us from a burning building. Or he could have fought off a bear that was attacking Sissy. Some way or another he would have been a hero dog.

He wasn't any hero, though. Mack was just plainly and simply a good dog. He loved me, and he was smart, and he was loyal. Most of all, Mack was there when I needed him and when Daddy needed him.

And that was enough.